THE GOBLINS AND THE GRAVEDIGGER

—a forgotten Dickens—

The Goblins and the Gravedigger

—a forgotten Dickens—

Novella

by

KENNETH L. CHUMBLEY
and
TONYA CLARKSON MCCAIN

Adelaide Books
New York / Lisbon
2019

THE GOBLINS AND THE GRAVEDIGGER
—a forgotten Dickens—
Novella

By Kenneth L. Chumbley
and
Tonya Clarkson McCain

Copyright © by Kenneth L. Chumbley

Cover design © 2019 Adelaide Books

Published by Adelaide Books, New York / Lisbon
adelaidebooks.org

Editor-in-Chief
Stevan V. Nikolic

All rights reserved. No part of this book may be reproduced in any
manner whatsoever without written permission from the author except in
the case of brief quotations embodied in critical articles and reviews.

For any information, please address Adelaide Books
at info@adelaidebooks.org

or write to:

Adelaide Books
244 Fifth Ave. Suite D27
New York, NY, 10001

ISBN-10: 1-950437-42-6

ISBN-13: 978-1-950437-42-9

Printed in the United States of America

to Jim McGuiggan

one to whom I owe so much

Kenny

to my fourth-grade art teacher, Mrs. Schmid:

thanks for letting me hang out in the art room during recess.

Tonya

Contents

Evening *13*

Midnight *39*

Cock Crow *63*

Morning *75*

About the Author *81*

Ah, for a man to arise in me,
That the man I am may cease to be.

Tennyson
Maud

Evening

"My, what frightful weather!"

It was the night before Christmas, and Samuel Pickwick was looking out a frosted window. Mr. Pickwick, retired businessman and acclaimed founder of The Pickwick Club, was staying at Manor Farm in Dingley Dell, the home of Mr. Wardle and his elderly mother. Arabella Allen, Mr. Wardle's lady friend—a pleasant young woman who secretly (desperately) hoped Mr. Wardle would save her from the tarnish of old maidenhood (she had, after all, already reached the advanced age of twenty-one!)—was also present. It was a time of stagecoaches, roast beef, and Yorkshire pudding; a time when women wore bonnets, pubs served pints, and children were called "darlings"; a time when folks were of a fine nature.

"Snows, does it?" asked Wardle.

"I should say!" replied Pickwick. "It's an old English blizzard we're having. The clouds slouch lower, the wind blows stronger, and the snow drifts higher. It's a rough night out, Sir—the kind that makes a fireside warmer when you sit by it."

"What'd he say?" shrilled Wardle's mother. The old lady was deaf when she wanted to be, and she employed an oversized ear trumpet to aid and abet her ruse. "Tain't anything a'matter is there?"

"No, Mother," Wardle half-shouted into the end of her trumpet. "Mr. Pickwick says a storm's afoot. Very cold. Strong wind. You can hear the weather rumbling in the chimney."

"Sounds like the Christmas Eve night when the goblins snatched Gabriel Grub," replied the mother.

The mention of *goblins* caught Pickwick's ear. "Who? What? Goblins?"

"Pay Mother no mind," chuckled Wardle. "She's referring to a story folks round here used to tell about a sexton— the church gravedigger—who was said to have been carried off by goblins. It's the kind of silliness with which we entertain ourselves out here in the country."

Even though he wasn't talking loudly or speaking into her trumpet, Mrs. Wardle heard every word and thwacked her son's leg with her cane, eliciting a loud "OUCH!"

"*Silly* ye say?! Ere anyone fool enough to doubt it? People 'round here are too sensible for silliness!"

"Very well, Mother," grimaced Wardle. "I's a *true* story, Mr. Pickwick"—his sarcasm was good humored—"and that's the end of it."

"No, that's not the end," rejoined Pickwick, "that's the beginning! Do tell us the tale, Mrs. Wardle."

"That son o' mine knows it perfectly well! Let 'im tell it!" she grumped.

Pickwick's and Arabella's eyes swung to Wardle. When Arabella chirped, "Please, Mr. Wardle, tell us! I'd love to hear about the goblins!" the rules of romance left him no route of escape.

"Oh, all right. I guess this is as good a night as any for a fairy tale"—old Mrs. Wardle gave her son a glance that was a warning shot across his bow—"I mean, *Christmas* tale.

"So let's see . . . where to start . . . ah, yes . . . I'll begin at the beginning!

"Ever so long ago, when our great-grandfathers lived and believed it . . ."

"Which means it's true!" interjected Mother Wardle.

"Yes, Mother . . . when our great grandfathers lived and believed it, there occurred a most curious incident.

"Winter gales do ghostly things to an old church. The storm will seek to gain entry through any window, door, or crevice it finds. And once inside"—Wardle's voice took on an eerie inflection—"it wails and howls as it stalks the aisles, glides around the pews, and creeps along the walls. It was a ghostly night to be in the old church, much less in its graveyard, but in the cemetery there was a solitary figure digging a grave in the light of a lantern.

"Earlier in the day, a short, unpleasant meeting had been held in the church between the digger and two deacons—typical ecclesiastics who had a whiff of phylactery about them."

"It's a mystery to me," ventured Deacon One, "how a divine like Brother Grub could have a ne'er-do-well son like Gabriel."

THE GOBLINS AND THE GRAVEDIGGER

The deacons, like many church officials, were decent men who possessed a considerable sense of their spiritual superiority, which gave them a cold severity toward smudged souls like Gabriel Grub, the church sexton.

"I remember Brother Grub well," recalled Deacon Two; "twice to church on Sabbath; thrice if he could. No one sang louder or prayed longer! What a shame to lose him before his three-score and ten."

"Do you remember what happened? Wasn't it an accident . . . at home . . . on Christmas Eve?"

"I believe you're right," said One.

Suddenly, without a rap or a tap, the door flew open, and in walked a man with a long nose, a long chin, scraggly hair, and no smile. It was Gabriel Grub, the one the deacons had just disparaged.

"Ah, Sexton," piped up Two, "so nice of you to drop by."

Grub sat down across the desk from the deacons and with undisguised irritation snarled, 'I didn't drop by; I were told to be here."

"Yes, well, thank you just the same," replied Two. "As you know, each year this time, it's customary for the deacons to distribute gifts of appreciation to the church help."

"Yeah, so?"

Two looked at One.

"So," said One, "it's with regret that we must inform you there will be no gift for you this year."

Grub sat bolt upright. "Wha'd I just hear? I's getting' no money? An' why's that? I know fer a fact the collection baskets been brimmin' o'er of late."

"Money's not the problem," said One.

"Then what is?" Grub demanded.

His tone was threatening, and the churchmen were rattled. They shuffled their papers, squirmed, looked up, looked down, looked around, looked everywhere . . . except at Grub.

Finally, Two cleared his throat, "The problem . . . Sexton . . . is you."

Grub shot to his feet. "I? What do ye mean, 'I's' the problem!?"

"There've been complaints," said One. "Parishioners are upset; they claim it's always a jolt and a jar when they must deal with you to arrange a funeral. You're perceived as being ill-mannered, intimidating, and insulting."

"So?" said Grub.

"The complaints have been so numerous and insistent that they merit action."

"Idiots! Both of ye!" flared Grub.

"Now Sexton, please, calm down. After all, we're allowing you to retain your position, which, considering the severity of the charges, is a most generous concession.

"But it would be a betrayal of the congregation's trust," and here One was particularly nervous, "if we overlooked your disrespects *ad infinitum*. Your father was a saint, a pillar in this church, and out of respect to him, we wish to give you every consideration."

Grub bristled. "Me father? A saint? Ha! Is bein' stupid a requirement for bein' a deecun?"

"Mr. Grub!" Two shot back, but Grub cannoned more loudly,

"Are ye finished?"

THE GOBLINS AND THE GRAVEDIGGER

"Yes," said One, meekly.

With that, Grub turned and stomped out, knocking over his chair in the process.

"Merry Christmas, Sexton, and a Happy New Year!" both deacons shouted.

"Pack o' muck to the two of ye . . . ad finitums!" Grub flung over his shoulder.

"How unsettling," said a shaky Two after Grub had slammed the door behind him.

"Indeed," noted One, "but we must tread lightly here, Deacon; good gravediggers are hard to find."

"At the time the situation at the church was unfolding," explained Wardle, "another situation, germane to the story, was occurring in a poor cottage in the village."

"Yer far from healthy, Mrs. Britain." The village doctor had been called to the Britain home and had just finished listening to Mrs. Britain's chest with his wooden earpiece. "I don't wanna scare ye, but there's nasty stuff about—plagues, poxes, fevers, the waste—'ave been fierce o' late. Diseases can resemble one another in the early stages, an' it's too soon fer me to tell if you've somethin' what's come to stay or is just passin' thru.

"Either way, stay in bed, an' try to keep as much water in ye as ye can."

"Plague?" Mrs. Britain asked, weakly.

"An' poxes, fevers, and an' the waste," added the doctor.

"Since sickness don't observe Christmas, I'll be by to check on ye tomorrow."

"Thank'ee, Doctur." Mrs. Britain sounded very tired.

As the doctor was heading for the door, Ben, Mrs. Britain's only child, pulled him aside and quietly asked, "Is she as bad as your look says, Doctor?"

"I'm never one to take a gloomy view of any patient's situation, but it's a sore business wi' yer mama. Fer now, I'm prescribin' prayer—pray 'er constitution's strong enuff to fight off what e'er she's fightin'.

"There's others I mus' see. Find me if she worsens."

"I will, Doctor. Thank you."

Returning to his mother's side, Ben asked, "How are you feeling, Mother? I think I need to stay home today."

"Ye'll do no such thin'," said Mrs. Britain in a voice that was more a sigh than a scold. "I'll not 'ave ye worrin' o'er me; ye've thins to do, and ye ought to be at 'em."

"About Christmas, Mother, I meant to get you something, but . . ."

"If'n ye wanna giv' me anythin', jus' stay the son ye are. Keep grace in yer 'eart and be faithful . . ."

"Unto death?"

"*Unto life.* Now, off wi' ye. I'll not 'ave ye in a fettle! I's feelin' a pinch better."

Ben laid his hand on his mother's head. "You've got some fever. I'll be home as soon as I can."

Ben leaned over and kissed her. After collecting the tools of his trade—the entirety of which consisted of a shoeshine kit—he left, careful not to slam the door.

"Might anyone like to pause for some tea or bread pudding?" asked Wardle.

"Save eatin' fer tomorra!" said his mother. "This ain't no place to stop unless yer wantin' another thumpin'!"

"Yes, Mother," replied her son with feigned fright. "But if anyone grows weak from lack of nourishment," Wardle smiled broadly, "I'm not to blame!"

"Onward!" ordered Pickwick.

And onward Wardle went.

"Fancy, if you will, that which is better than any treasure found at the tail of a rainbow . . . to wit, *first love*." (Arabella eagerly, and Pickwick sagely, nodded assent; Mrs. Wardle's face could have soured milk.) "First love is the only magic wand there is, for it's the love that's like no other. And oh, the miracles it can work; stunning miracles! like making a fool of one who isn't a fool by nature."

When Wardle cast a quick glance at Arabella, she blushed.

"Now Ben Britain . . . what a smart young spark he was! Poor as winter hay, but rich in all things good. Every girl what saw him was ready to fall in love with him.

"But for as long as Ben could remember, his heart was meant for Marion.

"Ah! bonny Marion, with her golden hair and green eyes—fairy eyes, some would say—that had the dazzle of the sun in them. And her smile had the power to melt all hearts. She was the pride of the shire, that girl.

"An' though she'd never spoken it, she loved Ben as much as he loved her."

"Hurry up, Marion," implored Gracie, Marion's best friend. "We're late to meet Alfred and Ben. They're going with us to Evensong, then to the party afterwards, and we must scoot!"

Marion was sitting at her vanity, combing her hair. Dreamily she asked, "Isn't love a lovely thing, Gracie?"

Gracie let out a small groan. "Love? We don't have time for you to get spoony; we're late!"

"Now don't you pout around me!" Marion was too much in love for Gracie's frowns to leave a dent in her ardor. "Just because your romantic life seems deprived of sunshine doesn't mean I must share your gloom. You love *love* as much as I do."

"Loving love isn't the same as having someone to love. It's easy for you to coo when you've got a boy like Ben," muttered Gracie.

"But you've got Alfred," Marion returned; "you've been keeping company with him for some time."

"I know, and Alfred's all right as far as he goes; he just doesn't go very far; he's a bit shy on gumption."

"Maybe you're underestimating him," encouraged Marion; "maybe you could be the making of him!"

"Maybe. He does have good intentions, but they need sharpening. If he'd get up and go, I'd likely get up and go with him, but I'm becoming an old maid waiting for him to show some initiative."

"Gracie! I can't believe the time you're wasting with your head in the clouds spooning on about Alfred," Marion teased. "We've no time to flutter; step lively!"

Forgetting that she wasn't the one making them late, Gracie jumped up, threw on her coat, and followed Marion out the door.

The storm still blew in Dingle Dell, but those inside Manor Farm were cozy and gave it no mind; they were too caught up in the tale being spun.

"Shoeblack!" Ben hawked. "Make your boots look new for only tuppence. Boots shined for Christmas!" What little money Ben made, he made by shining boots and shoes.

"Hallo! There you are, Ol' Man!" Alfred, Ben's best friend and the one keeping company with Gracie, rushed up. "Did you remember we're to meet the girls?"

"Hi, Alfred. Yes, I remembered, but I can't go. Mother's sick, and I'm worried sick over her. The doctor was by this morning, and he wasn't encouraging.

"Even if she wasn't sick, I'd need to stay here and work if mother and I are to have any Christmas tomorrow. Yesterday, I spent all I had on a gift for Marion."

"You did what?! You bought Marion a present? How could you do such a thing? I didn't get anything for Gracie; she'll scob my nob for sure when she sees Marion got something, and she got nothing. How could you do this to me?!"

Ben had a good laugh at this.

"So, what'd you get her?"

"Back in the fall, Marion and I walked by Pumblechook's merchandise store, and there was a red cloak displayed in the window. She didn't say anything, but she stopped and lingered for a long time, which told me all I needed to know."

Albert interrupted, "I've always admired how you're quick to figure out women."

THE GOBLINS AND THE GRAVEDIGGER

"Uh, thanks," said Ben. "Anyway, I asked if she wanted it, and she said, 'You can't afford something that pricey, Ben Britain! And besides, It's too grand for me.'"

"I wish Gracie thought that way."

"I so wanted Marion to have that cloak. But she was right about the price . . . it was an awful sum."

Alfred philosophized. "A woman is an odd mechanism; once she sets her mind on something, she can be as unreasonable as the stupidest man."

Ben ignored this and continued. "Well, I determined she'd have it regardless of the cost. So, I started saving—mostly pennies, an occasional silver—and finally pulled together five pounds. I bought it yesterday. It took every penny, but it was worth it."

Alfred groaned. "Ohhhh, this isn't good. What if I buy Gracie something pricey and she gives me the go by?"

"That's the risk love takes, my friend."

Alfred groaned again. Half in jest, half in worry, he said, "You've put me in a pickle! Some friend you are! I must dash and come up with something . . . something stunning . . . something feminine . . . something romantic. I wonder if Gracie needs a new chamber pot?"

As Alfred scurried off, Ben went back to work.

"Shoeblack! Make your boots look new for Christmas! Shoeblack! Tuppence."

A gentleman doing some last-minute shopping walked up and handed Ben two pennies. Ben knelt down on one knee and went to work. While the man read his paper, Ben gave each boot a shine the equal of any to be had in England.

25

When he finished, the customer inspected the job, reached into his waistcoat, and pulled out another penny.

"Splendid job, my boy! Merry Christmas to you!"

Doffing his cap, Ben said, "And to you, Sir! Merry Christmas to you!"

Just as the gentleman left, Marion and Gracie arrived.

"There he is, Marion. Hi Ben, Merry Christmas! Where's Alfred? He was supposed to meet us."

"He was just here but had to leave to see about something he'd forgotten."

"Merry Christmas, Ben!" enthused Marion. "I've been so anxious to see you! After Evensong, we're invited to the Perrywinkles for games, wassailing, and caroling. It's going to be a wonderfully fun evening!"

"Hi Marion! I've been anxious to see you too. And I'd love to go to the party tonight, but I can't. Mother is sick, and I need to be with her."

Marion was crestfallen, but Gracie wasn't taking "No" for an answer. "Oh, Ben, come with us. Your mum'll be fine. You've been working hard of late and could stand some Christmas cheer."

"There's nothing I'd like better, Gracie, but the doc says there's nasty stuff about, and I'm scared to death something bad's gotten hold of mother. She's very frail . . . and there's no one else to sit with her.

"Tonight, will you lift a glass of wassail to her?" he asked. Then, turning to Marion, he continued, "And will you think of me? If mother is better in the morning, I'll see you tomorrow for sure."

THE GOBLINS AND THE GRAVEDIGGER

"Oh, Ben, I'm heartbroken about this evening and will be even more so if we can't see each other on Christmas Day. But I do understand. Would it be alright if we popped by on our way home after the party?"

"Oh, yes, please do. I'll be looking for you!"

Gracie's impatience was getting the best of her.

"We'll say a prayer for your mum, Ben. Come on Marion, let's find Alfred. No telling what he forgot; probably his head. Merry Christmas, Ben!"

Wardle's tone took a serious turn.

"Everyone in town was afraid of Gabriel Grub (some more, some less), and after leaving the meeting with the deacons, he wandered about the village. Although thoroughly unkempt outwardly, Grub wasn't malformed, but inwardly, he was utterly deformed by hatred and bitterness. All who met him seemed to sense this, and they instinctively kept their distance. Not long after Marion and Gracie left Ben, Grub, who'd been roaming the town since his meeting with the deacons, wandered upon Ben and decided to vent some invective."

"Says . . . ain't you the Britain boy?"

"Yes Sir, I am."

With the sneer for which he was known, Grub jabbed, "Word's around town that there's some sickness at yer house that might soon require me perfessional services."

"THAT'S ENOUGH, GRUB!" boomed Mr. Tugby, the butcher, who had just stepped out of his shop. Anyone hearing him would have known his bite was the equal of

his bark. "Now clear out of 'ere, afore I do somethin' me religion might frown upon."

Grub, who knew better than to pick a fight with Tugby, turned and left. "Bah! And hooey on both of ye," he groused as he sulked off.

"'E's a nasty one, 'e is," Mr. Tugby muttered. "Pay 'im no mind, Ben."

"Say, it's gittin' late; come in 'ere and warm yerself. I's seen ye out 'ere all day in the cold, an' on Christmas Eve, no less!"

Ben accepted the offer. As he entered the shop, Mr. Tugby went behind the counter and produced a cup and a small jug.

"Ye need somethin' sizzlin' to warm ye up! Here, take a swaller o' this."

The butcher poured a darkish liquid into the cup and handed it to Ben. Taking a sip, Ben reacted violently, spraying the brew out his nose . . . coughing, wheezing, and gasping for air. When he could finally speak, he sputtered, "What"—cough, gag, sputter—"was that?"

"Tha', me boy"—Mr. Tugby paused here to take a drink from his jug, after which he smacked his lips—"is me special blend. *Goblin's Guzzle* I calls it; makes ye feel balmy inside!"

After taking another big swallow, the butcher asked, "What tomfoolery were Grub talkin' 'bout you needin' 'is services?"

"Mother's sick, Mr. Tugby. I don't know how Mr. Grub found out, but truth is, he's right; I may need him before long."

"What ails 'er?"

"The doctor's not sure. Maybe nothing serious; but she's so weak . . . Doc said there's bad stuff about."

"Don't think the worst, Son. It's pro'bly somethin' common, an' she'll be better afore ye know it. When life's a burden, ye've got to carry it like a man."

"Yes, Sir," said Ben, wiping his eyes with his sleeve.

"Before I left this morning, I told mother I hadn't money to get her a proper present. She said all she wanted for Christmas is that I keep grace in my heart and be faithful . . .'"

"Unto death?" interposed Tugby.

"Unto life," Ben related.

The butcher solemnly nodded. "She's a saint, Ben."

"She is. And I'd like us to have a decent meal tomorrow, even though there's no presents to put under the tree."

Pointing to a small, dressed fowl hanging on the wall, Ben asked, "How much for that partridge, Mr. Tugby?"

"That particular bird, my young friend, is a bargain at one bob."

Ben reached into his pocket and pulled out the few coins he'd earned that day from shoe shining.

"A bob?" He looked again at the change and closed his hand. "Twelve pennies?" Again, he opened his hand and looked at the coins.

Closing his hand again, he said, "May I have a clutch of tripe, Sir?"

"Tripe?!" Tugby nearly burst. "Did ye say, *tripe*? Ye'd dine on the lining of a cow's stomach—the most wicked article of consumption this island produces— at the very time the dying year calls 'is friends 'round 'im and prepares to pass away? Don't ye know tripe's the most wicked

THE GOBLINS AND THE GRAVEDIGGER

article of consumption this island produces? Not on me life will I send ye from me emporium wi' nothin' but tripe!"

Mr. Tugby took down the bird Ben had asked about. Wrapping it in brown paper, he put it in a sack. Ben started to protest, but the butcher shushed him.

"Not a word outta ye, young man! I'm not finished. Any Christma' meal worth its holly and ivy needs oysters." After scooping some of these delicacies into the sack, Tugby asked, to no one in particular, "Where'd I put that pease pudding?" Finding it on the shelf behind him, he cut a substantial slab, wrapped it and placed it in the sack with the partridge and oysters.

Ben again wiped his eyes with his sleeve. "I don't know what to say . . . here's all I have."

"Keep yer money, Son. But tonight, afore ye close yer eyes, send up thanks to the One who made the poor rich, the brokenhearted whole, and the captives free.

"Now, git home; it's gittin' dark, and I feel it in me bones that snow's acomin'. Merry Christmas to ye, Ben. May tomorrow be a glad day fer ye, even though a shadow seems to hang o'er it."

"Thank you, Mr. Tugby! For me and my mother, thank you!"

"With his load lightened by a kind man's kindness," continued Wardle, "Ben headed for home."

"I'm so enjoying this," gushed Arabella. "I can't believe it's nothing more than a fairy tale."

31

Mrs. Wardle heard this and, of course, had to comment. "It tis more than a fairy tale! And if'n that son of mine says it ain't, he'd best stay outta my reach."

Grub lived in a fusty, ramshackle shack that was lit only by the candleshine of a single wick. As soon as he returned home, he grabbed his flask, and after several gulps, sat down, put his head on the table, and was soon emitting boozy snores. But no sooner had he fallen asleep than there came a knock at the door. When it didn't rouse him, the knocking turned to pounding.

"Huh? Wha'? Hang it all!" Grub mumbled as he regained consciousness. "Who's there? Ye don't have to bring the door down!"

Stumbling to the door, he opened it to find two villagers without, shivering.

"Winkle? Snodgrass? What'er ye fools doin' here?"

"Mr. Grub!" spoke Winkle, "thank goodness you're home. It's freezing out! May we come in?" Grub made no move to invite them in, but they shoved past him anyway. "We assure you, we wouldn't be here were it not an urgency."

"Oh yes, Winkle is quite right," said Snodgrass. "Of course, we'd rather be home, Sexton, but an unanticipated urgency brings us out."

Snodgrass leaned over and took a big sniff. "Is that liquor I smell? Mr. Grub! Are you drunk?" "To the knees maybe, but no higher. Now, state yer bizness; me patience is about run out."

"There's been a death," said Snodgrass, "resulting in a corpse."

THE GOBLINS AND THE GRAVEDIGGER

"Most deaths result in a corpse!" sneered Grub. "Stash the body behin' yer house; it'll keep jus' fine in this weather." Shoving his visitors toward the door, Grub added, "Come back when it's warmer."

Winkle put his hands on both sides of the door and refused to be budged further. "We can't wait that long."

"An' why not?!"

"Because," explained Snodgrass, "the deceased died of the plague—cholera—which can remain in the remains after death. It wasn't two hours ago that a constable from several shires away came to the house and left a body belonging to a distant relative of my wife. Apparently, when the records were searched for the deceased's next of kin, she was determined . . . regrettably . . . to be the one. The village where he died was anxious to be rid of his earthly remains, thus, the missus and I have found ourselves with a most unwelcomed . . . chore . . . er . . . responsibility."

"Most unwelcomed!" opined Winkle. "And as the passing was due to plague, it's pressing that the body be inhumed."

"Be wha'?" puzzled Grub.

"Buried," answered Winkle.

"In ground froze hard as rock!" snapped Grub.

Snodgrass stood his ground. "I am sorry, Mr. Grub, but you are the church sexton, and my wife and I are members in good standing, and we need a grave dug, and I'd hate to have to speak to the deacons about this, and . . ."

"Spare me yer threats," interrupted Grub, "and git out. There'll be a hole fer yer stiff in the morning. Maybe ye two'll git wha' got him and take 'vantage of me Christma' special: three graves fer the price of one."

33

Snodgrass and Winkle looked at each other, shuddered, and exited, but not without first dispatching, "Merry Christmas" over their shoulders. "Bah!" was all they got back before the door slammed shut behind them.

Grub was sullen. "I's nothin' else to do; might as well git this done. Where's me flask?" Putting on his grimy coat, frayed scarf, and sexton's hat, Grub grabbed his shovel and lantern, took a swallow from his flask, and headed out.

"If anyone is interested, I'm confident a dram of elderberry wine can be found." Wardle wasn't tired of talking, but he thought his audience might need an intermission. To his amazement, Pickwick and Arabella urged him to continue.

"As you know, there are some who consider preachers barely less sacred than the book they preach, but such adulation rarely attaches itself to a sexton. Gravediggers tend to be . . . abnormally developed . . . higgledy-piggledy misfits . . . which shouldn't surprise, seeing how regularly they're reminded of their mortality.

"But Gabriel Grub went beyond the normal gloom for a gravedigger. He was a most unhappy man. And nothing made him unhappier than Christmas cheer."

Night was heavy and snow was falling as Grub stumbled out. His trek to the cemetery sorely tempted his diminished soul, for along the way he saw and heard Christmas life everywhere: the sound of sleigh bells, carolers, the glad light of fireplaces reflected through cottage windows, the shouts of neighbors wishing each other "Merry Christmas," and the savory aromas of geese being roasted and pudding being boiled.

All of which made him hiss like a green log thrown on the fire. He would have been happier to have seen children sick with fever, or measles, or croup, or whooping cough, for in those cases, there was always the chance his professional services might be needed.

Despite the numerous irritations, he scuttled on, heading for the path to the cemetery known as Coffin Lane. By now it was snowing heavily, and Grub's head was down.

As was Ben Britain's, who was coming from the opposite direction headed for home. Not seeing the other, they brushed in passing, but Grub reacted as if he had been waylaid.

"What's this outrage?!" yelled Grub. Squinting through blood-shot eyes, he recognized Ben. "Is that you, Britain?"

"Yes, Sir; beg your pardon . . . oh . . . Sexton, it's you. I'm most sorry, Sir; didn't see you; had my head down against the snow. I'll be on my way. Merry Christmas to you!"

"Beg me pardon? Sorry? Merry Christmas? Ye think to dismiss yer assault agin' me that easily?"

Some of it was the liquor talking; most of it was Grub's characteristic vileness.

"Yer not man enuff to speak fer himself earlier, so ye let a meat cutter speak fer ye; and now yer not man enuff to owe up to what ye jus' did. It's time ye were taught some manners."

Before Ben could reply, Grub did something unspeakably brutal. Dropping his spade and lantern, and without warning, he delivered a crack with his fist to the left side of Ben's head. The blow caused Ben to drop all he carried and left him too staggered to speak. A second time Grub struck, delivering another blow to the right side of Ben's head, dropping him to his knees.

"Please, Sir, whatever I did, I'm sorry."

The acrimony within Grub continued to rise like a mist of malignity that bordered on madness. Rage, like love and fortune, blinds; Grub could no more see the depravity in his actions than he could see the backside of the north wind. Swiftly, unconsciously, the fury of his anger rose to a crescendo. Grabbing his spade, he delivered a vicious strike to Ben's back that drove him to the ground, senseless.

"You give me a wide berth from now," shouted the sexton, "except when ye need me perfessional services."

Smiling pure spite, He collected his implements and left.

There's no telling how long Ben lay on the ground, but later that evening, his mother heard a fumbling at the door, as if someone was trying t o get in.

"Son . . . be that you?" whispered Mrs. Britain.

Slowly, the door opened, and Ben staggered in— holding a bloody ear with one hand and clutching the sack containing Christmas dinner with the other. Without speaking, he dropped the sack and collapsed on the floor.

Mrs. Britain was so weak, you would have barely heard her pitiful scream even if you'd been standing next to her.

Midnight

Once again, Wardle paused, "Does anyone need a stretch?"

"Heavens, no!" enthused Pickwick, as he raised his arms above his head and stretched. "It's a smashing good story; please proceed at flank speed!"

"Is 'e still callin' it a *fairy* tale?" Mrs. Wardle demanded to know.

"No, Mother Wardle," Arabella answered, "he's not even hinted that."

"Then why did 'e stop? Pick it up!" croaked the matriarch.

Wardle smiled and resumed.

"Upon reaching the graveyard, Grub set down his lantern and began stabbing away at the frozen dirt. Snow was falling, and the air was freezing, but his flask kept him going. Soon, he was singing."

Brave lodgings for one, brave lodgings for one,

A hole of cold earth, when life is done;

A stone at the head, a stone at the feet,

A rich, juicy meal for worms to eat;

Rank grass overhead, damp clay All around,

Brave lodgings for one, in this holy ground.

No one else would have liked it, but Grub quite enjoyed his ditty.

"What a thought"—he paused to take a swig from his flask. "A Christmas fun'ral . . . they should wrap the coffin with a red bow! Ho! Ho! Ho!"

"HO! HO! HO!"

Grub paused mid-swig, not sure of what he heard. It sounded like a laugh, but it wasn't his laugh. He looked around. The graveyard was full of shadows, and frost hung tight to the tombstones, but except for the swish of the snow, not another sound was there; sound itself seemed to have frozen. He wasn't unnerved, but he was uneasy.

"Is someone there? . . . Must have been an echo," Grub theorized.

"IT WAS NOT!" came a voice like a thunderclap.

And then came whisperings, stirrings. "There he is! . . . Hunt him! . . . Haunt him!"

Suddenly, Grub saw—maybe just felt—a dark shadow flit by, and he stood rooted to the spot as the starch left his spine.

"Who . . . who's there?"

"Turn around and you'll see."

Sometimes, fairy folk provoke more curiosity than alarm, but what Grub saw when he turned around made his blood run cold.

For seated on a tombstone was a strange phantom. His long legs, which might have reached the ground, were crossed in a quaint fashion, and his hands rested on his knees. He wore a bright green, close-fitting garment trimmed in gold brocade. A short cloak dangled from his back. On his head was a pointed hat—the kind known as a *sugar-loaf* hat—garnished with a long feather. His shoes curled up at the toes, and he looked as if he'd been sitting there comfortably atop the tombstone for two or three hundred years. It was a goblin, grinning as only a goblin can grin, and the sight drew from Grub a disquieting gasp.

"Who . . . are you?" Grub sputtered.

"Just a friend and neighbor!"

Grub was now more scared than he'd ever been in his life and was reduced to stammering.

"Neigh . . . neigh . . . neigh' . . . "

"Spit it out, man! You sound like a horse. *Neighbor! Friend and Neighbor!*

If you call me an elf or an imp,

I might give your noggin a crimp!

Call me a fairy . . .

You'll find me contrary,

—the goblin here leaned in to make what he said next more impressive—

So watch what you call me, you shrimp!

Grub turned to run, but found himself surrounded by dozens and dozens of sniggering goblins, who appeared out of nowhere. Everywhere he looked, his way was blocked.

"What brings you out this night?" the goblin asked in a stern way.

Grub stuttered, "A g-grave, Sir. I's here to dig a grave."

"Who makes graves when others make merry?" the goblin shouted.

"gabriel grub! gabriel grub!" chanted the gaggle around him.

"What's in the flask, gravedigger?"

"B-Brandy, Sir. I admit, it's smuggled; you're not here to collect the excise on it, are ye?"

"Fiddle-dee-dee!" twittered the goblin. "Who drinks on a night like this?"

Like a choir, the goblins chorused, "Gabriel Grub! Gabriel Grub!"

The goblin looked long and hard at the trembling man, and then, raising his voice to the sky, shouted, "Whom do we take as our fair and lawful prize?"

The answer was like the surge of a church organ: "GABRIEL GRUB! GABRIEL GRUB!"

Grub shrieked!

Leaning his head back, the goblin let out an unearthly screech. Kicking out his feet, he admired his curled-up shoes and asked, "Have you anything to say, gravedigger?"

"It's . . . it's . . . very curious, Sir," replied Grub, one hand pressed to his forehead, the other held over his heart. "But it could be the spirits I's seein' are from the spirits I's drinkin'."

At this, the goblin gave Grub a kick that bowled him over.

"Has anything from a bottle ever given you a kick like that?" chortled the goblin.

"OWWW!" groaned Grub.

"Who thinks what he's seein' comes from a bottle?"

"GABRIEL GRUB! GABRIEL GRUB!" yelled the assembly.

THE GOBLINS AND THE GRAVEDIGGER

"My friends seem to know you, gravedigger . . . they seem to know you well."

"Beggin' pardon, Sir, but I don't know how they'd know me; we've ne'er been introduced.

And then with some insolence in his tone he asked, "An' e'en if they do, wha' gives ye the right to question me 'bout me bizness?"

It was the wrong question.

"RIGHT? YOU DARE TO ASK ME ABOUT MY RIGHT? What gave you the right to beat a boy senseless the night before Christmas? HOW DARE YOU CHALLENGE MY RIGHT TO QUESTION YOUR WRONG!"

The goblin then cut loose a scream that reverberated off every surface. Throwing his legs into the air, he stood upside down with the tip of his hat atop the tombstone, and then, with extraordinary agility, executed a somersault that left him directly in front of Grub.

Grub's tongue could hardly move. "I . . . I mus' be goin'," he said as he turned to leave.

"Going? HO! HO! HO!"—he was mocking Grub—"The gravedigger says he must be going!"

Suddenly, the lights in the church flashed a pale yellow, the organ whorled out unearthly music, and the bell in the tower clanged wildly. As Grub's brain reeled, a menagerie of goblins formed a circle around him. They capered and skirled in a wild frenzy, displaying acrobatic dexterity as they jigged and danced and leapfrogged over tombstones and each other.

"The only place you're going," said the goblin, "is with us!"

45

Before Grub could react, the goblin grabbed his collar and sank with him through the earth.

In the rapidity of the descent, Grub lost his breath. When he caught it, he found himself in a large, subterranean hall, such as the old legends associated with the dwarves. The light was neither black night nor bright noon but more like the gloaming, when twilight releases the shadows that have been prisoned up all day. Looking around, Grub saw the same gob of goblins he'd seen in the graveyard. Before him, sitting on a throne carved from a large rock, was the one with whom he had been conversing.

Grub's fear had now multiplied six times larger than it had been on the surface.

"Welcome to our humble home, gravedigger! Look around, and you'll see why I'm in charge."

Grub looked around but saw nothing that provided a clue to what the goblin was saying.

"Isn't it obvious?" the goblin asked. "It's because I'm 'the fairest of 'em all'!"

After the slightest pause, every goblin present howled with merriment. Some laughed so hard that they fell on their backs and kicked their feet in the air. One goblin with a big belly laughed until he coughed . . . then coughed until he choked . . . and then choked until other goblins slapped his back to get him breathing again.

"My, but it's cold enough to take the skin off your face," said the goblin. "Bring me something sizzling!"

At his command, a small, officious-acting goblin, who seemed a court attendant, disappeared and strutted back with a goblet full of what looked like liquid fire. As the goblin drained the cup, a red-hot glow was seen descending his throat.

"Ah!" cried the goblin, "makes me feel balmy inside! Bring a bumper for our guest."

"Thank ye, but I's not in the habit of taking anything warm at night."

"Then you need a new habit," countered the goblin.

While one goblin held him down, another held open his mouth, and another poured the aqueous brimstone down his throat. The whole assembly howled with laughter as Grub choked, gagged, and wiped away tears that gushed from his eyes.

"Boys," sighed the goblin, "our hospitality doesn't seem appreciated by our guest. Have we anything else to offer?"

"Hot tar!" "Ball and chain!" "His head!" were shouted out.

"His head?" mused the goblin. "An intriguing thought! The only problem . . . is that a beheading is over so . . . quickly. But still, an idea whose time may come."

Looking Grub squarely in the eye, the goblin asked, "Do you know why we brought you here, gravedigger?"

"Because yer trolls, the lot of ye!"

There was a collective gasp as the entire company lurched back.

"Trolls? I assure you, we're not trolls. I'll admit we're romps. I'll even admit we're capable of being a bit naughty."

"We might tap on your windows," shouted out a goblin, "or spill your milk."

"Or hide your sheep," cackled another.

"Or untie your water bucket and let it fall into the well," sniggled a third.

"But," continued the goblin, "we're not even our step-mother's half-brother's fifth cousin to trolls! We dread those misfits as much as you!

"So guess again why you're here."

"To rob me of me life, I'd wager."

"No, no, no; I told you, we're not trolls! And since you're such an abysmal guesser, I'll tell you why you're here.

"You're here, because it's Christmas, and we've a gift for you.

"This caught Grub totally off-guard. "A gif'?" he puzzled.

"That's right."

"What'd ye mean, a 'gif'?"

"I mean something you desperately need."

"I don't know what yer talkin' about."

"Then let me elaborate," said the goblin.

"I've been on your scent for some time and have learned two things about you. First, your heart is hollow; there's no holy of holies in you."

"A pack o' muck," said Grub.

"Second, in your eyes I see a story no one who knows you has ever read.

"But I've read it, and because I've read it, I've a gift for you."

Grub let out a scornful cry.

"I doubt you've given much thought to how wretched you are, but you will tonight; the boys and I will see to that."

"Yer daft!" gnarled Grub.

THE GOBLINS AND THE GRAVEDIGGER

"You tempt me to leave you to your fate, but I shall do my best to resist temptation."

"Yer beyond daft," clacked Grub.

Looking about the cavern with a broad, grinny smile, the goblin asked, "What have we for this pathetic man, boys?"

"*The Book*! *The Book*! *The Book*!" came the answer.

"Ah, yes!" crowed the goblin, "*The Book*!"

"The Book?" Grub puzzled.

"Was that an echo?" the goblin asked? "Yes, gravedigger, *The Book*! A one-of-a-kind, hot-off-the-press, never-to-be-forgotten, first-edition, copyright-pending book."

"Ye can keep it!" Grub was riled, but he sounded ridiculous—and the goblins all giggled.

"We can't keep it; it's not ours, it's yours!

"BRING IN *THE BOOK*!"

The goblins parted, and the same small, officious goblin walked in carrying a very big book. Striding imperially to the stone throne, he stood rigidly at attention, awaiting further instructions.

The goblin spoke. "Here's your book. See, it has your name on it."

"I ain't a reader," said Grub.

"Not a problem, because you don't read this book, gravedigger, you look at it. It's an enchanted book that acts like a mirror. People don't look at mirrors to look at mirrors; they look at mirrors to look at themselves. And your book, just like your mirror, will reveal yourself to yourself . . . in only three pages!"

"Bah!" Grub repeated.

THE GOBLINS AND THE GRAVEDIGGER

"Why only three pages? I'm glad you asked. "Every book, gravedigger, has but three parts: a beginning, an ending, and an in-between. And every life, like every book, has the same three parts. Thus, your book has a page for your *past*, your *present*, and your *passing*.

"I'll venture you weren't expecting such a wonderful gift for Christmas!"

"An' I'll venture I's reporting ye to the sheriff fer sexton-napping!" Grub's face was set like grease in a dish.

"It seems your brandy-bought courage hasn't quite evaporated yet.

"You're a wreck of a man, and this night, you're going to see yourself for who you are!

"We'll start with your past, not because it can be bent out of its eternal shape, but because what you are now is tied to what happened to you then.

"SHOW HIM THE PAGE FROM HIS PAST. And if he won't look, squeeze his head till his eyes pop out."

Just as the goblin anticipated, Grub refused to look. The goblin nodded and a large goblin stepped out of the crowd, grabbed the back of Grub's head, and shoved it down until his eyes were on the page.

"Look carefully, gravedigger," said the goblin, "and tell me what you see."

Had Grub been struck by lightning, he could not have received a greater shock. Gasping, he uttered, "It's . . . me . . . as a boy . . . and me father!"

"You sound alarmed, gravedigger. Why would the sight of your father disturb you?"

"Before I continue," informed Wardle, "I must warn you that what I am about to relate is disturbing and involves matters not usually discussed in mixed company."

"We're all adults here," said Pickwick. Arabella nodded in agreement. "Do go on," directed Pickwick.

What Grub saw was an older man—angular, long-faced, stern-looking—sitting in a winged-back chair and reading from a large Bible he held on his lap. A boy of about eight was in front of the fireplace playing with his wooden soldiers. As Grub looked on, the picture suddenly came to life.

"Behold, the Lord cometh with ten thousand of his saints to execute judgment upon all . . ."

Young Gabriel sneezed.

"Hallo? What was that?" the man asked.

"Nothing, Father," said the boy.

"Nothing?"

"I only sneezed, Father."

"Sneezed, you say? Then why did you say it was 'nothing'? A sneeze is *something*, is it not?"

As the father rose from his chair, the boy knew from past experience what was coming . . . and he began to whimper.

"Why did you prevaricate by saying *something* was *nothing?*"

Without another word, the man delivered a vicious slap to his son's head.

The boy's pain and weeping were heartbreaking. "Please, Father; I'm sorry . . ."

A second blow was next delivered to the other side of Gabriel's face. The poor boy fell to his knees and sobbed.

THE GOBLINS AND THE GRAVEDIGGER

"Stop sniveling you worthless cob."

Raising his cane, the father hammered it down on his son's back, driving him to the floor.

"As Grub remembered, the old panic and fear came on him like a phantom," explained Wardle.

"In public, me old man was the picture of piety—spoke of God, read his Bible, church-goin' . . . things tha' have the ring of the devout about 'em. But fer all his religion, he weren't the better fer it. Ye never knew when he'd rage. Anythin' could set him off; nothin' could set him off. He never needed cause to beat me.

"Why're ye showin' me these things, forcin' me down paths where I don't wan' to go?"

"Why? Because you're walking the same path as your father."

"I AIN'T!" shouted Grub.

"YOU ARE!" returned the goblin.

"There's more on the page, gravedigger; look again."

Reluctantly, Grub did, and another drawing materialized. It was the same room as before, but now, a sparsely adorned Christmas tree stood in the corner, and holiday decorations were on the mantle. But there was something else . . . Grub's mother and father were in the room having an argument. Once again, the photo became animated.

"Please, Dear," sobbed the woman, "I'll not mention it again."

"You're right, woman; you'll *not* mention it again!" said the husband as he violently slapped his wife across her face.

53

The poor woman slumped to the floor, dazed, nearly unconscious.

Gabriel had just walked in and seeing what happened screamed out, "MOTHER!"

"Get out," snarled the fiend, "this doesn't concern you!"

Rushing to the fireplace, Gabriel grabbed the iron poker. Holding it above his head, he advanced toward his father.

"I told you to get out!" the man ordered.

Gabriel drew closer.

"Put that down and leave, NOW!"

Gabriel took another step closer.

"I said, PUT IT DOWN!" As the man stepped back to distance himself from his son, he tripped over his fallen wife. In falling, his head struck hard against a table. There was a dull, hollow moan . . . then nothing; the man lay on the floor and never moved again.

Gabriel hovered over him, still holding the poker. For a fleeting second, he thought to put the matter beyond all doubt. But he didn't. At length, he dropped the iron and went to help his mother.

"Why must I see this?" Grub's voice was increasingly desperate. "Why are ye conjurin' up these ghosts?"

"You didn't kill your father, gravedigger."

"God knows I wanted to," Grub allowed.

Continued the goblin, "You've seen your share of the worst, gravedigger, and you've every right to be angry. But anger is a ticklish thing. It releases into the soul tremendous . . . *steam* . . . that can be used to drive a hammer or pat an egg. Some use anger's *energy* to rise above their wounds—if only

THE GOBLINS AND THE GRAVEDIGGER

to let their scourge know they're unbroken. But others are ruined by it—the anger caused by a monster itself becomes a monster that drags victims to self-destruction."

"I's heard enough of yer mush," spat Grub.

"I don't think you have" There was sting in the goblin's reply. "I think you need to see the next page in your book.

"SHOW HIM WHAT IS! SHOW HIM HIS PRESENT!"

Grub was desperate. "No, please . . ."

The little goblin turned the page, but Grub wouldn't look. Again, the larger goblin grabbed the scruff of his neck and forced him to see.

The drawing on the page was of Ben Britain lying unconscious on the floor of his home, with his seriously ill mother on the floor beside him.

"Do you recognize him, gravedigger? The boy you beat earlier this evening?"

Grub turned defensive. "He'd been impert'nent; tried to knock me down as I were out on sexton bizness. He needed to be taught a lesson."

"NO HE DIDN'T!" stormed the goblin. "It was an accident, a jostle, a bump; no harm done, nothing further required. Yet, you took something as harmless as a sneeze and did to an innocent boy worse than your father did to you!

"It's bad enough that you're bent on destroying yourself . . . must you destroy others as well?!"

In a hoarse whisper, Grub asked, "Is he dead?"

"What if he is; death is what keeps you in business, is it not?"

For the first time, a note of contrition crept into Grub's voice, 'Please . . . don't let him die."

"I have no control over that," answered the goblin, solemnly.

As Grub looked on, a knock at the door of the Britain house was followed by a badly warbled verse of *Deck the Halls*. When no one answered, the singing stopped and the knocking increased.

"Ben? Mrs. Britain? Anyone home?" The voice was Marion's. "We've some fruit cake from the party for you."

After a few seconds, the door opened an inch and Alfred's head peeped in. As soon as he saw what he saw, he let out a cry and flew inside, with Marion and Gracie right behind.

"Help us," implored Mrs. Britain, who could barely speak.

When Marion saw Ben bloody and unconscious, she screamed.

Again, Grub implored, "Please, don' let him die."

The little goblin was so upset by the thought of what Grub had done to Ben that he delivered a stout kick to the sexton's shin, eliciting a loud squall of pain.

"Your cruelty," spoke the goblin, "is the cause of what you're seeing."

"Cruelty? That I caused?

"Jus' what do ye know of cruelty, goblin?! What do ye know abou' havin' a father who'd as soon beat ye as look at ye? What do ye know abou' the nightmare of seein' him smash in yer mother's face? What do ye know about bein' so alone, ye've no heart on which to rest yer head? What do ye know abou' the hell I's carried inside me because of wha' was done to me?" Grub was crying. "TELL ME, GOBLIN, WHAT DO YE KNOW ABOU' ANY OF THIS?!"

A tear dropped from the little goblin's eye.

For the longest time, the goblin didn't speak; sometimes, wisdom shows itself in silence.

"What do I know? I know that the boy you saw laying on the floor was there because of you! I know that, gravedigger! And I know nothing that happened to you justifies what you did to him!

"The facts are undeniable, yet you still resist them. Which means you must see the last page . . . THE PAGE OF YOUR PASSING."

Grub was sobbing. "No, I can't bear it; I beg you . . ."

"SHOW HIM!"

The little goblin turned the page, and Grub looked without being forced.

The drawing he saw was of black night and a black hole that was an old, abandoned house that reeked of damp, and mold, and filth. Two men were pictured walking to the front door, bearing on their shoulders what looked like a body wrapped in burlap. The man in front carried a lantern. For a final time, the drawing on the page changed into an actual scene.

"'Tis a cold Christma' Eve, eh, Mate?" said the man in front in a strong Cockney accent.

The man behind, with a matching dialect, replied, "Aye. And I twern't be out at all, 'cept fer me wife screechin' about' havin' nothin' decent fer Christma' meal.

"'What abou' the odds and ends I put in the cupboard,' I says, 'the muffins and crumpets I found behin' the baker's? Scrape off the mold, and they's as good as new.'"

"Wha'd she say?"

"Not much. Jus' started flailin' at me with the skillet and said if'n I didn't come up with somethin' proper fer Christma' meal, she'd knock me into next year. I's only here cause I's in no hurry to git to next year."

"Ye let yer woman squawk at ye like that?" scolded the man in front? "Yer an embarrassment to husbandry, ye know it?"

"Maybe so," said the man behind, "but it's too late to undo it now."

When the man in front pushed on the front door, it creaked open, and the two stepped into the house's decrepitness.

"What the deuce!" said the man behind. "This place smells worse than stinkin' meat.

"Say, why's we bringin' the body 'ere anyway? Why ain't we takin' it to the cem'tery?"

The man in front answered, "The deacons said they weren't allowin' the scoundrel to be buried in holy ground, so they's payin' us to dispose of 'im on the cheap, an' there's nothin' cheaper I know o' than this."

"Ye've lost me."

"We's leavin' 'im fer the rats," the man in front explained, "this place is crawlin' with 'em."

This caught the man behind totally by surprise. "Rats?!"

"They'll 'ave 'is bones picked clean afore we git 'ome. An' I've a bag of cheese curds to sprinkle on the remains . . . priming the pump, ye might say."

THE GOBLINS AND THE GRAVEDIGGER

"This is givin' me the creeps!" said the man behind who had a low tolerance for such nefariousness. "If ye 'adn't been late meetin' up, we'd be done already."

The man in front offered an explanation. "I meant to be earlier, but just as I's goin' out the door, me woman tells me I ain't goin' nowheres till I'd plucked the squab fer the pigeon-pie we's havin' fer Christmas dinner and pitted the cherries goin' in the puddin'."

The man behind couldn't quite believe he'd heard what he'd just heard. After the longest pause, he asked (with a note of scorn), "Ye were late cause yer woman made ye stay 'ome to pit an' pluck?"

"Correc'. I weren't about to light her fuse the night afore Christma'; what kind of idiot do ye take me fer?

"Let's dump Grub and clear out o' here afore the rats think we're their dinner."

A gasp from Grub bounced off the cavern walls. "Grub?" he asked frantically. "Did he say *Grub?*"

"I believe he did," answered the goblin. "But let me check with the boys.

"What'd he say, boys?"

"Grub! Grub! Grub!"

"That's what I heard," agreed the goblin.

Hearing this, there arose in Grub the dread of a coming evil that left him agonizing in an anguish from which he saw no escape. "So tha's how I end? No mourners, no coffin, no preacher sayin' a good word o'er me . . . jus' rats?"

"Saying a good word? And what would that good word be, gravedigger?"

Grub hung his head and trembled. The cavern was in total silence.

"There ain't none," confessed Grub. "I've squandered me life . . . I's nothin' to die on."

"Nothing to die on? Who told you that?" shot back the goblin.

"Ye jus' showed me how I..."

The goblin cut him off. "What I showed you is what shall be if you continue to anger your life away.

"But remember this and remember it to the last—so long as there's life, there's hope."

Grub fell to his knees, shaking like a leaf.

"Hope . . . ye's sayin, fer me . . . hope?"

"You're awfully unloveable," said the goblin; "and many will count it a good day when you're gone. But there's more mercy in heaven and earth than you've ever dreamed. If the sand caked to the bottom of your boots can be thrown into the fire to make a crystal through which the stars can be seen . . . there's hope, gravedigger, even for you."

It was as if a thousand thunders went off inside Grub. Few things in this world are stronger than hope, and suddenly, unexpectedly, incredibly there it was being held out to him! In what had just seemed total darkness, the sexton now saw a faint ember that shone like a floodlight and brought him to his knees. In new-found humility he asked,

"But how, goblin? How can I escape the rats . . . and the end I deserve?"

"The answer to that is the easiest but hardest thing I could ever tell you, gravedigger: you must *love*."

"Love? What do you mean?"

"I mean you must live and die as if another's life is more precious than your own. You must show devotion, humiliation, submission, service, trust, and belief to those who favor you, wound you, or tear your heart to pieces.

"To live lovingly is a long, hard road, but it alone can conquer the ghosts that haunt you and free you from a past that holds you. It's a task and a trudge, but it's within your reach, gravedigger."

For what seemed forever, Grub stood silent, his head bowed.

"I've been ripped up this night."

"What's that?"

"I've felt more grief thinking of what I am this night than I ever felt before."

"Splendid!" said the goblin.

"Ye've taught me, Sir."

"The dickens you say! And just what have I taught you?" The goblin leaned forward and cupped his hand to his ear, awaiting the answer.

"That I's been a bloody fool.

"In however many days are left me, I means to spend 'em unselfing meself!"

Springing from his throne, the goblin removed his hat and with a flourish made a deep bow to the sexton and said, "Your servant, Sir."

The cavern darkened. First, the goblin, then the rest, stepped back into shadow . . . and were gone.

And Gabriel Grub, utterly spent, laid down on the ground and fell sleep.

Cock Crow

"Gabriel Grub had never known a night so long, so short, or so significant," said Wardle. "When he awoke, it was Christmas morning, and he discovered he was still in the graveyard where he'd been the night before. He was covered with snow. His flask lay nearby, as well as his spade and lantern. The grave remained half dug. Everything was as it had been, except there were no goblins to be seen."

"Wha'? . . . Where?" Grub groaned in the dawning light. Retrieving his flask, he turned it upside down and shook it. Nothing came out. 'I mus' 'ave gone too deep into the spirits las' night."

Starting to rise, he suddenly paused. "No! Wait . . . spirits . . . the book . . . me father . . . Ben Britain . . . rats . . . THE GOBLINS!"

The peal of the solitary bell in the church spire made up in quality what it lacked in quantity and triggered another thought in Gabriel's thinking.

"Hope! Tha's wha' the goblin said; so long as there's life, there's hope. An' I's alive! An' it's Christmas!

"THERE'S HOPE, THERE'S HOPE, THERE'S HOPE!"

"Had you seen Gabriel at that moment," commented Wardle, "you would have thought him seized by hysterics. He took no heed of anybody or anything. He ran about like a child. He scooped up handfuls of snow and threw them in the air, leaving him so covered with the frozen moisture that he began to resemble a snowman. He laughed and cried in the same breath. He was, at that moment, the embodiment of pure joy."

"Wait . . . love . . . the goblin said another . . . more precious than me. Yes!"

Before he could think another thought, Gabriel headed for the village as quickly as he could. There was something that couldn't wait.

In the Britain home, Ben was still laying unconscious on the floor. Alfred had gone looking for the doctor but unable to find him, had returned. He and Marion kept quiet vigil beside Ben, tormented by the fear of not knowing if he would live or die.

Just about the time Grub awakened in the cemetery, a groan slipped from Ben's lips.

With a start, Marion asked anxiously, "Ben? can you hear me?"

Slowly, Ben opened his eyes and murmured, "Was I hit by a train?"

Ben's mother heard this and whispered, "Ben? Is it ye I hear?"

THE GOBLINS AND THE GRAVEDIGGER

"Yes, mother; but, Owww, I hurt all over."

Marion had ten thousand questions, beginning with, "What happened?"

Ben was trying to clear his head. "I . . . Mr. Tugby . . . on the way home . . . dark, snowy . . . I . . . bumped into someone . . . uh . . . the sexton, Mr. Grub. And . . . and . . . he hit me." Ben pointed to the side of his head. "And he hit me again. After that . . . I don't remember."

Alfred blazed. "Grub? The sexton did this?" Alfred jumped up and started pulling on his coat. "I'll find him, and when I do, I'll wring his neck!"

"Hold it, Sir Galahad," said Gracie, "he'll kill you."

"He might," agreed Ben. "Thank you, Alfred, but it's best we stay away from Mr. Grub."

Gracie spoke again, genuinely. "You're so brave, Alfred."

"But you just said Grub would kill me."

"I didn't say you were smart, I said you were brave."

While matters inside the home seemed on the rise, a solitary figure had crept up to the house and was peeking in a window, trying to assess the situation.

When Ben felt he could, he got up and went to his mother.

"It must have scared you terribly to see me come in last night."

Mrs. Britain's only response was to look into her son's eyes and smile. She seemed so weak.

Ben leaned over and kissed her.

Marion had been waiting patiently but could contain herself no longer. Taking Ben's hand, she pulled him away

65

THE GOBLINS AND THE GRAVEDIGGER

from the bed. Looking into his eyes, she said, "All night, I feared I would never be able to tell you something I've wanted to tell you forever."

"What's that?"

"It's . . ." Marion, suddenly shy, lowered her eyes, "it's that I love you.

"I'm not saying I understand all I'm saying. I only know that when I'm with you, the sun is brighter; and when we're apart, I never hear music.

"But last night . . . oh, Ben . . . I've never been so scared."

A romantic "Awwww," unconsciously eased out of Gracie's lips. Looking peeved, but without looking at him, she asked Alfred, "Are you paying attention?"

When Alfred answered, "To what," Gracie gave him a sharp elbow in the ribs.

Ben saw no one else in the room but Marion. But now it was his turn to be shy, and he blushed up to his eyes as he said, "I've something for you."

This caught Marion off-guard. "Something for me?"

"Alfred, that package in the corner? Would you hand it to me, please?"

Alfred saw a package wrapped in brown paper. He retrieved it and handed it to Ben, who handed it to Marion with the apology, "I hadn't money for nice wrapping."

Marion was uncomprehending, caught completely by surprise. Haltingly, she undid the paper and found the red cloak she'd seen in the store window.

"BEN!!"

Gracie now looked at Alfred with a decidedly peeved look that said, "Are you sure you're getting this?" This time,

67

Alfred adamantly nodded a nod that meant, "Yes, I understand perfectly."

"But how?" Marion stammered. "You can't afford this!"

With a smile, Ben replied, "Well, I can assure you I didn't steal it. Do you like it?"

Marion started crying.

"What's wrong?" asked Ben, totally surprised.

After a big sob and a swipe of her nose with her sleeve, Marion sputtered, "What's wrong? You don't know what's wrong? How could you not know?!

"What's wrong is, I've nothing for you. You know I've no money; how could you do this to me?"

In exasperation, Ben turned to Alfred, "That's what you said!"

Marion didn't stop. "It didn't bother me that I had nothing for you when I thought you had nothing for me . . . but you've something for me when I've nothing for you.

"And I feel terrible!"

Considerable boohooing followed.

Gently embracing her, Ben whispered, "Tell me something."

"What?" came back the whimper.

"Do you think I love you so little that I wouldn't love you at all if you didn't have a present for me?"

Marion blubbered, "Did you say that you . . . love me?"

"Beyond telling."

"Oh Ben, your love is the dream I've hoped for forever."

Said Ben, "Marion, out of this whole world, you're the only one I want to be mine."

It was like both—Ben and Marion—were standing in a flood of sunshine so dazzling and bright that it blinded

THE GOBLINS AND THE GRAVEDIGGER

them to everything, except its own radiance. Nothing else was said between them—just an embrace and a kiss—which said all that needed to be said.

As she watched, Gracie was momentarily lost in romance, but her peevishness soon returned. "Are you picking up on this, Alfred?"

"Indeed, I am, my dove!"

Gracie suddenly turned playful. "In that case, Freddie, what'd you get me?"

"Get you?" replied Alfred. "Oh, yes, get you . . . After all, it is Christmas, a gift-giving time, so, naturally, it's to be expected that I got you something.

"As to that . . . may I ask . . . could you use a new chamber pot?"

"A CHAMBER POT?! YOU GOT ME A CHAMBER POT?! The gods themselves won't be able to save you if you got me a chamber pot!

"I didn't say I got you a chamber pot," protested Alfred.

"And thank the gods you didn't!"

"I will, the next time I see them," said Alfred.

"But as for what I got you," Alfred was fumbling in his coat. "How about this?"

He pulled from his pocket a small box, which he handed to Gracie. Only a very few gifts can fit into a small box, but Gracie was too startled to venture a thought as to what the box she held contained. When she opened it, she was (for the only time in her life) struck dumb. She looked at Alfred, then at the box, then at Alfred again, and then took out a gleaming diamond ring. As diamond rings go, it was quite modest—actually, it was very modest (it

69

was miniscule). But despite its diminutive size, another first for Gracie occurred—for the first time ever, her eyes were filled with starlight and the hunger in her heart was gone. To Gracie, her ring looked as big as any of the queen's crown jewels.

Alfred dropped to his knee, took Gracie's hand, and, in a noble voice asked, "Gracie, will you marry me?"

When Marion saw the cloak, her *shriek* was easily one of the finest shrieks ever heard. But compared to Gracie's *scream*, Marion's shriek was but the croak of a frog. Gracie dropped to her knees and threw her arms around Alfred's neck at the very time he tried to memorialize the moment with some lines of poetry.

> If yet I have not all thy love,
> > I shan't ever have it all.
> > > I cannot breathe another sigh,
> > > > nor entreat a tear to fall.

Suddenly, his arms flailing, Alfred gasped, "Gracie! Let go! I can't breathe!"

Gracie didn't lessen her chokehold, and Marion couldn't resist. Leaning in, she whispered in Gracie's ear, "There you go getting spoony again."

"Shut up, Marion," said Gracie, her arms still tightly wrapped around Alfred's neck.

Outside, still peeking in the window, the onlooker thought, "I . . . don't understand. I thought the goblin indicated the boy would . . . but he seems fine."

THE GOBLINS AND THE GRAVEDIGGER

Just then, the reverie of the young people was interrupted by a knock on the door.

"Probably the doctor," said Ben, "come to see about mother."

When Marion answered the door, it was Mr. Tugby, not the doctor, who was standing there.

"Merry Christmas, everyone! I 'ope ye don't mind me poppin' by, Ben. Ye and yer mama's been on my mind since I saw ye yesterday, and I thought I'd check to make sure Christma' Day were bright fer the Britains."

When the sexton saw it was Mr. Tugby, he made his peeking even more inconspicuous.

"Mr. Tugby! Come in, Sir," welcomed Ben. "All is well! And we've special cause for happiness, for Gracie and Albert are just now engaged!"

Gracie held out her ring hand, and Mr. Tugby oohed and aahed until Alfred glowed, mentally patting himself on the back for his contribution to the morning's euphoria.

But just then, the reverie came to a dead halt.

For Mrs. Britain made a sound. Only it wasn't just a sound, it was a rattle—the kind you never want to hear.

All heard it . . . and froze. When Ben looked at his mother, he knew. Hurrying to her side, he placed his ear on her chest and kept it there for the longest time. He didn't move; he couldn't move. His world had stopped.

"My mother's dead."

Outside, Grub gasped like he did when he heard about the rats. Had those inside not been so preoccupied with the situation, they might have heard him. As it was, they didn't.

71

Instinctively, Gabriel Grub knew what Mrs. Britain's death meant for him. Once word got around about what he'd done to Ben, he knew he'd be blamed for Mrs. Britain's death. When an inferno rages, the air can become so hot that the wise thing is to back off until the flame has burnt itself out. Grub knew this must be his course of action, even though he knew of no place that would afford him refuge.

Creeping quietly to the front of the house, he took a small sack from his coat pocket, placed it in front of the door, and slipped away.

Ben sat on the bed beside his mother for the longest time. Marion sat behind him, her head against his back, silently weeping. Alfred and Gracie huddled together, eyes wet, arms around each other. Mr. Tugby stood in a corner, his head bowed in solemn sadness.

When Ben spoke, what he said came as a shock. "Grub killed my mother."

Marion sat up and said, "Ben, you can't say . . ."

"QUIET!" No one had ever heard Ben speak so harshly.

"I could overlook what that foul man did to *me* . . . but not this . . . I can't overlook this. Mother was barely alive as it was . . . the shock of seeing me last night was more than she could bear."

Rising to his feet, and to no one in particular, he said, "I've something to do."

As he was putting on his coat, Alfred piped up, "I'm coming with you."

Marion, thoroughly frightened, grabbed at Ben's hand, but he jerked it away and headed for the door.

THE GOBLINS AND THE GRAVEDIGGER

"Wait," pled Gracie, "listen. I know I'm flighty and that what I say often goes in one ear and out the other . . . but Ben, whatever you're intending, you can't."

Ben reached the door and raised the latch.

Mr. Tugby spoke.

"I never would've believed it, Ben."

Ben paused and in a tone of irritation said, "Believed what?"

"That ye would break yer promise to yer mama."

"Break my promise to my mother?" the irritation deepened. "It's Grub I mean to break."

"Then maybe I heard ye wrong. I thot ye told me ye promised yer mama ye'd 'keep grace in yer heart an' . . . I's forgotten . . . what else were it she said?"

Mr. Tugby had just given Ben a blow harder than any he received from Grub. For a moment, Ben couldn't move; he was frozen by conviction.

In a low voice Ben answered, "Be faithful unto life."

"Aye! Tha's it. Ye promised ye'd keep grace and faith in yer heart unto life. An' here ye are, with a chance to honor tha' promise, and yer unwillin' to do so.

"Wha' yer thinkin' o' doin', Ben, ain't because yer wicked; it's cause, right now, yer weak. But the fruit o' weakness can be as bad as the fruit o' wickedness.

"An there's somethin' else what needs to be said. If'n ye merely try to bury what yer feelin' this hour, yer feelin's will only get stronger. Somewhere along the way, they'll break loose and sweep you before 'em like a flood. The only way ye can avoid drownin' in 'em is to live the grace of which yer mama spoke and let be wha's happened be as though it

73

never happened. Anythin' short of this, Son, will be to yer own ruin."

No one could see the battle raging inside Ben, but the battles he fought thereafter were nothing by comparison. Just when evil was about to take him captive, the goodness that was his essence fanned by the wisdom of a humble butcher, pulled him back, and the anger and hatred and vengeance slowly drained out of him.

When he again spoke, everyone knew that Ben—the Ben they'd always known—was back. "I need to find the undertaker" was all he said, but how he said it said more than what he said.

As he walked out the door, he stumbled over something lying on the ground. Picking up a small sack held closed by a drawstring, he stepped back inside. Opening it, he looked in, and then looked up, utterly astonished. Upending the bag, a small pile of gold coins spilled onto the table. Last of all fell out a note on which was scrawled the words, "Compliments of the goblins."

Morning

Late on Christmas morning, Winkle and Snodgrass trudged up to the church cemetery. They'd been to Grub's lodging, but not finding him, they looked for him in the graveyard. When they arrived, they found a half-dug grave but no gravedigger.

And they were perturbed!

"That rascal!" snapped Snodgrass. "I'll brook no more of his effrontery. Wait till the deacons hear about this!"

Gabriel Grub was never found because he was gone. His sorrow over the passing of Mrs. Britain was intense; he ached over the tragedy he had witnessed. But he rightly judged that the healing of Ben's sorrow was best left to the passing of time.

So he left with only the clothes on his back, but with every pocket stuffed with gold. Most malicious people are miserly, and Gabriel Grub was counted among this crowd. For years he hoarded his earnings, though he had no one to hoard for.

But now he was an altered man. He didn't know what was before him, but he knew he was going to make a break with what was behind him. And he did. He journeyed to a village where he was unknown, and there, love beat down hate.

And wonderful, startling, clandestine things began to happen.

Late at night, poor people, who hadn't money to pay their rent, would hear a knock at the door. When they answered, fearing it was the landlord there to evict them, all they'd find would be a small bag of gold coins with the note: "Compliments of the goblins."

Parents, with sick children but no money to pay the doctor, and widows, who had no family to help them in their infirmity, had similar experiences. There'd be a knock and upon answering, they would find a bag of coins and a note with the badly scratched words: "Compliments of the goblins."

In his redemption, Gabriel's expiation was uncomplaining, his repentance was genuine, his determination sincere. The memory of his night with the goblins never left him, and he rose to a height beyond himself. In time, the loveliest thing about Gabriel Grub was Gabriel Grub.

The village searched for him (but let it be said neither the deacons nor Snodgrass and Winkle searched very hard), but it was as if he had vanished into thin air.

At some point, someone suggested, purely as a joke, that goblins had grabbed him, and this gossip hadn't passed through four sets of ears before it was being told as sacred truth. The man who replaced Grub as sexton had a bit of charlatan about him, and he saw opportunity beckoning.

Before long, he had become a general book of reference about Grub's kidnapping and had turned it into a profitable sideline—exhibiting to the curious, for a modest fee, a good-sized piece of the church's weathervane, which he claimed had been accidentally kicked off by a one-eyed horse the goblins flew off on when they grabbed Grub. By extraordinary luck, so he claimed, he had found this indisputable piece of evidence in the churchyard following a fierce thunderstorm not long after he was employed by the church.

"And now I come to the last scene," said Wardle.

"Twenty years or so after Grub went missing, a gaunt old man came to town. He shuffled through the streets and lanes of the village and looked around . . . as if he was familiar with all he saw. At length, he entered a pub where were gathered some locals. After ordering a pint, he asked if anyone knew a Ben Britain."

"Ben Britain?" replied a customer. "Why, everyone knows Ben and Marion Britain. Two better ain't to be found."

"Good folks are they?" asked the stranger.

"I should say!" chimed in a second customer. "They're more than good, they're the best we got!"

The first man continued, "Some years back, Ben came into some unexpected wealth. Mos' woulda drained it on theirselves, but not Ben. No; he said, 'freely gained, freely given.' O'er the years, 'e and 'is wife 'ave 'elped many, I should 'ave ye know. When me Kelly needed docterin', the Britains paid fer it. They's somethin', they is!"

The second man asked the first, "Didn't 'is money come in about the time the sex'on went missin'?"

"Who went missin'?" asked the stranger.

"Our sex'on, old Gabriel Grub. Disappeared years ago. I's not suggestin', ye understand, that Ben got his money from Grub; 'e were a wicked one, Grub were, but the goblins finally got 'im."

"Goblins got 'im? How do ye know that?"

"How'd I know it?" asked the first man a bit indignantly. "Why, I seed with me own eyes the piece of vane kicked off by the 'orse the goblins flew 'im off on! Tha's 'ow I knows it. An' don't try to talk me outta wha' I's sayin' . . . I KNOWS WHAT I'S SEED!"

"The stranger smiled and rose to leave. Reaching into his pocket, he pulled out all it contained—a single gold coin, his last—left it on the counter and walked out into the gloaming, heading for a path known as Coffin Lane.

"Up it he went to the church graveyard. Finding the spot where he'd once spent a Christmas Eve, he stretched out on the ground, and with nothing but the stars for a blanket and a thought to die on, fell asleep.

"Sometime during the night, Gabriel awoke to see a brilliant, golden staircase . . . and he climbed it . . . right into the sunrise.

"When word got round that an old man no one knew had been found dead in the cemetery at daybreak, Ben Britain sent word he would put up the money to give the stranger a decent burial."

As some men were gathering up the old man's earthly remains, a curiously shaped figure, wearing a sugar-loaf hat, peeked out from behind a tombstone at the edge of the cemetery. Uncharacteristically, his eyes glistened, and in a whisper of a whisper he said, 'Your servant, Sir.'"

Off in the distance, though muted by heavy snow and howling wind, a church bell was heard striking one.

"Oh my!" said Wardle. "It's past midnight! I've slogged on far too long."

"It wasn't a slog, Sir," corrected Pickwick, "and it wasn't too long. It was a great story greatly told! Whenever a man breaks the grip of hate and turns to love, he covers himself in glory.

"But it is late and time for us to retire. And on the strength of this good story, let us go to our beds and dream cherished dreams.

"After all, it will soon be Christmas Day, in the morning!"

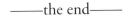

——the end——

About the Author

Kenny Chumbley is a minister, publisher, and the author of two illustrated children's books: *Ol' Pigtoes* and *The Green Children*, the Literary Classics 2017 Enchanted Page Award recipient for best children's storybook of the year. A series of short essays he has written on fairy tales have appeared in the on-line literary journal Modern Literature (modernliterature.org). In addition to his writing, he is the playwright, along with his coauthor, Jim McGuiggan, of *The Green Children* musical play, which premiered in the fall of 2017, and he is the playwright, along with his coauthor Tonya Clarkson-McCain, of *A Goblins Christmas Carol,* with lyrics by himself and original music by Kyle Shaw, DMA.

Kenny is a lifelong resident of the Illinois prairie. He holds a BA from the University of Illinois and an MA and MDiv from Trinity Theological Seminary. Most importantly, he is the father of Gary, Kelly, and Steve, and Grandpa to Maddie, Mia, Aniyah, Honor, Millie, and Wrigley.

Made in the USA
Columbia, SC
14 May 2019